This Little Tiger book belongs to:

_____

_____

_____

_____

For Nadia and Paul
~ A H B

For Tiziana and Sammy
~ J B B

LITTLE TIGER PRESS
An imprint of Magi Publications
1 The Coda Centre, 189 Munster Road,
London SW6 6AW, UK
www.littletigerpress.com

First published in Great Britain 2004
by Little Tiger Press, London
This edition published 2008

ISBN 978-1-84506-903-2

Printed in China
2 4 6 8 10 9 7 5 3 1

At the End of the

Rainbow

A H Benjamin & John Bendall-Brunello

LITTLE TIGER PRESS

"Wow!" gasped Badger and Fox.
"It's beautiful!"
A bright, clear rainbow
hung in the sky
like a jewel.

Badger and Fox stood gazing at the bright colors.

Then Badger said, "You know, there's treasure at the end of a rainbow!"

"What's treasure?" asked Fox.

"I'm not sure," replied Badger, "but I think it's gold or silver or jewels—something that will make you rich for ever and ever!"

"Let's go and find this treasure!" cried Fox excitedly.

And they were off, racing toward the nearby woods.

As the two friends hurried along
all they could think of was treasure.
   What did it look like? Was it big
or small? What color was it?
Just then they noticed Squirrel,
sitting in front of a pile of acorns.

"My treasure," he was singing to himself. "My beautiful treasure!"

Badger and Fox scampered up to Squirrel.

"Go away!" he ordered. "You're not stealing my treasure!"

"That's not treasure," said Fox, "that's just a pile of acorns."

"It's treasure to me," replied Squirrel. "It's my food for the winter. What's more important than that?"

"Well, we're going to find the real thing!" said Badger, and the friends raced off.

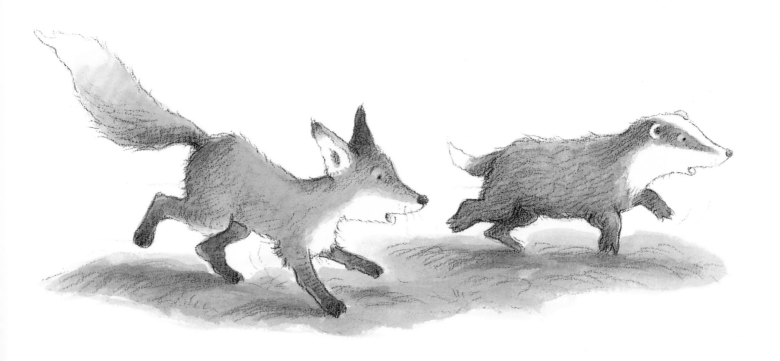

Soon Badger and Fox came to
a small river. Among the tall grass
they spotted Mother Duck.

"My little treasure!" she was calling.
"Where are you?"

Badger and Fox were curious.

"Are you looking for treasure?" they asked.

"Yes, my own little treasure," replied Mother Duck. "Oh look, there he is!"

A golden, fluffy duckling came pattering along. Mother Duck tucked him under her wing.

"Don't disappear like that," she said gently. "You'll have me worried, my treasure."

Badger and Fox looked puzzled.

"Is that your treasure?" they said.

"Of course," smiled Mother Duck proudly. "I love my baby more than anything in the world, so he is a treasure to me. Aren't you, my little one? Now let's go home."

Badger and Fox rushed on, eager to find their treasure at the end of the rainbow. They clambered up a steep, bumpy hill, and found Old Hare sitting at the top.

"Hello, there!" he greeted.

"Hello!" called the friends. "We're on our way to find treasure!"

"Ahh," nodded Old Hare. "I have lots of that."

"Really? Where?" they asked.

Old Hare patted his head. "Here," he said. "My memories are my treasure. They make me happy."

"What are memories?" asked Badger.

"They're all that you remember from the past," said Old Hare. "Things you've done, places you've visited, friends you've loved. Your adventure today will become a memory you'll treasure, one day. So enjoy yourselves, little ones!"

"Good bye!" called Badger and Fox. And they were off, sliding down the other side of the hill.

Just then thick, dark clouds filled the sky. The rainbow vanished. It started to rain, harder and harder. Badger and Fox had to take shelter.

"We'll never find our treasure now," said Badger miserably.

As they waited for the rain to stop, the friends remembered Squirrel. How happy he was just to have enough food. And Mother Duck and her love for her baby.

Old Hare was
happy too,
because he
had his
memories.
They all had
their own kind
of treasure ... Maybe treasure wasn't gold and
silver and jewels. It was what you loved,
something very special, and something that
made you happy.

Fox looked at Badger and Badger looked
at Fox ...

"You're a treasure!" said Badger,
jumping up.

"You're a treasure too," said Fox,
skipping around.

And they started laughing and
dancing until they could dance
no more!

At last the rain stopped and the sun came out again. The two friends happily made their way back home. Far, far behind them a new rainbow had appeared in the sky. But neither Badger or Fox noticed.

fantastic reads from Little Tiger Press

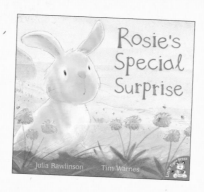

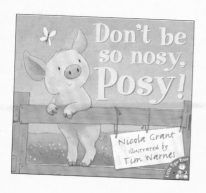

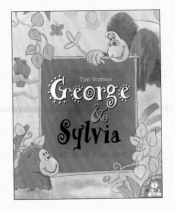

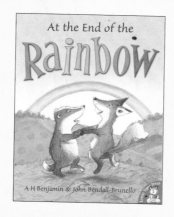

For information regarding any of the above titles
or for our catalogue, please contact us:
Little Tiger Press, 1 The Coda Centre,
189 Munster Road, London SW6 6AW, UK
Tel: +44 (0)20 7385 6333 fax: +44 (0)20 7385 7333
E-mail: info@littletiger.co.uk www.littletigerpress.com